For Jason

Bloomsbury Publishing, London, New Delhi, New York and Sydney

First published in the United States of America in 2014
by Bloomsbury Children's Books
1385 Broadway, New York, New York 10018

This edition first published in Great Britain in 2014 by Bloomsbury Publishing Plc
50 Bedford Square, London, WC1B 3DP

Text and illustrations copyright © Salina Yoon 2014

The moral right of the author/illustrator has been asserted

A CIP catalogue record of this book is available from the British Library

ISBN 978 1 4088 5837 0

Printed in China by Leo Paper Products, Heshan, Guangdong

1 3 5 7 9 10 8 6 4 2

www.bloomsbury.com

BLOOMSBURY is a registered trademark of Bloomsbury Publishing Plc

Penguin and Pumpkin

Salina Yoon

BLOOMSBURY

LONDON NEW DELHI NEW YORK SYDNEY

It was autumn, and very white on the ice, as always – which made Penguin curious.

I wonder what autumn looks like off the ice.
Let's go to the farm and find out!

Penguin's baby brother,
Pumpkin, waddled over.

Can I come and see autumn, too?

'I'm sorry, Pumpkin. But it's too far for a fledgling.'

Grandpa agreed. 'Maybe next year, Pumpkin.'

Penguin, Bootsy and their friends headed to the farm.

The journey was long, as Penguin . . .

looked . . .

and looked . . .

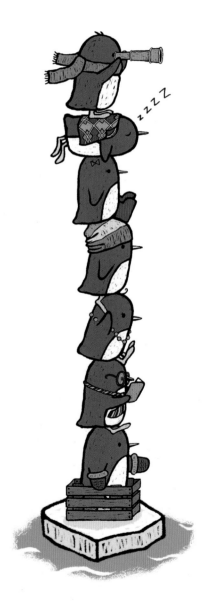

and looked for signs of land.

Finally, the penguins arrived.

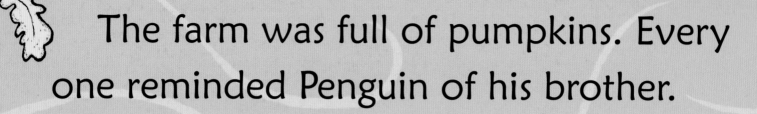

The farm was full of pumpkins. Every one reminded Penguin of his brother.

Then Penguin looked up.

The penguins each picked out a pumpkin.

Some were smooth.

Some were bumpy.

Some were long.

Some were curved.

Sweet dreams, dear pumpkin.

YAWN!

Every pumpkin was loved.

Penguin had a different idea.

They rode back home with
their autumn harvest.

The autumn explorers were excited
to share their treasures from the farm.

But where was Pumpkin?

Penguin found a clue.

What's this?

'What are you doing over here?'

'We imagined . . .

autumn on the harvest moon . . .

autumn on spooky Saturn . . .

and even autumn on the Red Planet!'

'You have a space-tacular imagination,' said Penguin.

'But I wish I'd got to see
what autumn REALLY looks like.'
Pumpkin sighed.

'See autumn?' thought Penguin.

'Wait right here, Pumpkin!'

Penguin took the crate up on to a cliff.

Grandpa and Bootsy followed a trail
of leaves that led them right to Pumpkin.

'A pumpkin for Pumpkin!
A perfect match!'

Thank you!

Penguin finally returned. 'What does autumn really look like?' asked Pumpkin eagerly.

'Look up!' said Grandpa.

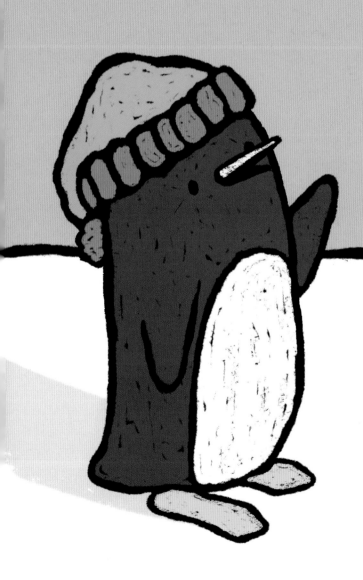

'Autumn looks like . . .'

'. . . snowing leaves!'